HOCUS FOCUS

DISCARDED

by Sarah Willson
illustrated by Amy Wummer

Kane Press, Inc.
New York

Acknowledgements: Our thanks to Nicole R. Fram, MD, Resident Physician, Wills Eye Hospital, Philadelphia for helping us make this book as accurate as possible.

Library of Congress Cataloging-in-Publication Data

Willson, Sarah.
  Hocus Focus / by Sarah Willson ; illustrated by Amy Wummer.
     p. cm. — (Science solves it!)
Summary: Jack and Gina let the teasing of a classmate stop them from wearing their glasses until a class field trip makes them change their minds.
  ISBN: 978-57565-136-1 (pbk. : alk. paper)
  [1. Eyeglasses—Fiction. 2. Peer pressure—Fiction.] I. Wummer, Amy,
ill. II. Title. III. Series.
  PZ7.A3174Hoc 2004
  [E]—dc22

                                                    2003011700

10 9 8 7 6 5 4 3

First published in the United States of America in 2003 by Kane Press, Inc.
Printed in Hong Kong.

Science Solves It! is a registered trademark of Kane Press, Inc.

Book Design/Art Direction: Edward Miller

www.kanepress.com

"Hey, Jack! Yoo-hoo, Jack!" called a voice. Jack knew it belonged to his friend Gina. But which of the fuzzy shapes getting off the bus was her? He had no clue.

"JACK!" said Gina. Suddenly she was right in front of him. "Do you want to come over after school today?"

Jack shook his head. "I can't," he replied. "I have to go . . . do something with my dad."

He didn't want to tell Gina that he had an appointment with the eye doctor.

"Do you have trouble seeing the chalkboard in school?" Dr. Romero asked Jack later that day.

"Sometimes," Jack admitted.

Dr. Romero examined Jack's eyes. Then she made him read letters on a big chart.

An eye doctor is called an ophthalmologist (opp-thal-*mol*-oh-jist). An optometrist tests eyes and prescribes glasses. An optician makes or sells eyeglasses and contact lenses.

Ops means "eye" in Greek.

"Well, Jack, you're nearsighted," Dr. Romero said. "It looks like you're going to need glasses." She wrote out a prescription, and Jack's dad took him to buy eyeglasses at the mall.

CROSS-SECTION OF THE EYE

Lens
focuses light rays on the
retina by changing shape

Optic Nerve
sends nerve signals
(vision message)
to brain

Cornea
clear tissue
that covers
the eye

Pupil
hole that
lets light
into the
eye

Iris
colored part of eye

Retina
turns reflected
light from what
you are looking at
into nerve signals

When all the parts of your eye work
right—you have good vision.

When you're nearsighted,
you can see things that
are near. But things that
are far away are out of
focus. They look blurry.

Jack wore his glasses to school the next day.

"Hi, Jack! Nice glasses!" said his teacher, Mr. Brenner.

"Gee," Jack thought. "I was hoping no one would notice."

Then Hank, a kid in Jack's class, walked by. "Hey, Four Eyes! Nice glasses!" he shouted.

Jack felt bad. He whipped off his glasses and headed into class.

"What's up?" asked Gina. "You look upset."
Jack showed her his new glasses.

"Oh," she said. She pulled a sparkly purple
case from her backpack.

"You have glasses, too?" exclaimed Jack.

Gina nodded. "But I never wear them. The
one time I did, Hank called me Four Eyes."

"I thought you could see great!" Jack said. "You always read the chalkboard for me."

"I'm farsighted," Gina told him. "I can see the board—no problem. It's just the close-up stuff that's all blurry."

When you're farsighted, you can see things that are far away. But things that are near are out of focus. They look blurry.

Jack decided he'd wear his glasses at home—*not* in school.

"I won't give Hank a chance to call me Four Eyes again," he thought.

Glasses for nearsighted people have concave lenses shaped like this.

Concave Lens

Glasses for farsighted people have convex lenses shaped like this.

Convex Lens

Jack and Gina made a good team. Gina could see everything Mr. Brenner wrote on the chalkboard. She told Jack, and he took notes.

Jack could do all the measuring in science.
He peered at the tiny numbers on the beaker
and read them to Gina.

One day Mr. Brenner pulled Jack aside. "Didn't I see you with glasses on last week?" he asked.

"Glasses?" Jack repeated. "Oh, *those* glasses! I don't need them all the time. Just for, uh, doing my homework—at home."

Jack started for the cafeteria. "Heads up!" yelled Hank. A volleyball bonked off Jack's head. "Ouch!" he cried. He hadn't even seen it coming.

✓ CHECK YOUR VISION
• I hold a book up very close when I read.
• I have trouble seeing the chalkboard.
• Some things look blurry to me.
• I squint a lot.
• Sometimes I cover one eye to see better.

If you said "yes" to one or more of these statements, you may need glasses.

The next day, the class went on a field trip to a rock quarry.

"Rock-hounding is a lot of fun, but you have to be careful," Mr. Brenner told the class. "Please pay attention to the signs. I repeat—OBEY ALL THE SIGNS!"

OFF LIMITS

"Let's go," said Gina, tugging on Jack's elbow. "I see a great rock pile over there."

All Jack could see was a blurry gray lump in the distance, but he followed after her.

CAUTION

Suddenly Gina tripped and went flying.

"Sorry," said Jack. "I should have warned you about that tree root."

They heard Hank laughing. "Gina, how are you going to find rock samples? You can't even see stuff that's right in front of you!"

Gina ignored Hank. "Come on, Jack," she said. "We're going to find samples that he can only *dream* of."

"Wait," said Jack. "This rock's pretty cool."

"It's not bad," said Gina. "But . . ."

Just then they heard Hank yell. "Mr. Brenner! Look what I found!"

Gina sprang up and slipped off her backpack. "You keep looking here, Jack. I still want to check over there." She hurried away.

Gina finally reached the rock pile she had spotted. There was a sign nearby, but the letters were a blur. She squinted, trying to make out what it said. She took a step backward, then another, and another, and . . . .

"Caution!" she read. But it was too late.

Do you have 20/20 vision?
20/20 means you can read a special line
(labeled 20 on the eye chart) from 20 feet
away. Not many people have such good
eyesight. More than 100 million people
in America wear glasses!

"Jack!" Gina shouted. "Help!"

Jack raced toward the sound of Gina's voice. He found her standing in a hole.

"I can't climb out," groaned Gina. "I tried, but the sides keep crumbling."

"Wow!" Jack was peering into the hole. "There are some great rock samples in there!"

"So what?" said Gina. "I'm going to get in big trouble for not obeying that sign—the one I was *trying* to read when I fell in here!"

Just then they heard Mr. Brenner call to the class. It was time to go!

"Now what do we do?" asked Jack in a panic.

"I have a jump rope in my backpack," said Gina. "Go get it, and pull me out of here. Hurry!"

Jack looked all over for Gina's backpack.
But everything was a blur!

He knew what he had to do. He took out
his glasses and put them on. Right away,
everything came into focus. There it was—
Gina's backpack!

Working fast, Jack tossed one end of the jump rope to Gina. He tugged and tugged. Finally, Gina scrambled out of the hole.

"You're heavier than you look," Jack said.
"I filled my pockets with rock samples while I was waiting for you," Gina told him.

Gina and Jack caught up with the rest of the class. Jack hoped Mr. Brenner wouldn't notice how out of breath they both were.

"Great samples!" Mr. Brenner said. "Those are the best I've seen all day!"

That night Jack thought about what had happened at the quarry. They could have gotten into trouble, or hurt—or both!

Jack decided he would wear his glasses from now on, no matter what Hank said. And he'd get Gina to wear hers, too.

Jack passed Hank in the hall the next day.
"Nice glasses," said Hank.

"Well, *I* like them," said Jack. "They're great for finding things—like the *best* rock samples!"

"I really mean it," said Hank. "Nice glasses." He gave a weak little smile.

Jack couldn't believe his eyes. Hank's teeth were covered with shiny new braces!

"Oh, I get it," said Jack. "You're afraid I'm going to make fun of you."

Hank's face turned red.

"Well, I won't call you Metal Mouth," promised Jack, "as long as you don't call me— or anybody else—Four Eyes!"

"Deal!" said Hank.

Jack spotted Gina down the hall. It was so great to be able to see things!

"Hey, Gina!" he called, hurrying to catch up with her. "You know, I really think you should start wearing . . ."

Gina turned around. "My glasses?" she said.
Jack grinned. "Exactly," he told her.

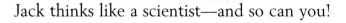

I can draw conclusions!

THINK LIKE A SCIENTIST

Jack thinks like a scientist—and so can you!

When scientists want to solve a problem, they gather information and draw conclusions. When Jack has trouble seeing the board, the doctor gives him an eye test and draws a conclusion—that Jack is nearsighted.

Look Back
What information are we given about Jack on pages 3, 15 and 17? What happens to Jack on pages 24 and 25? What conclusion does Jack come to on page 27?

Try This!
Draw a conclusion! Ask two friends the questions from the checklist on page 15. Which friend do you think has better eyesight?

Now check your conclusion. Copy the eye chart on this page onto a large piece of paper and hang it on a wall. Have your friends stand about 20 steps back from the chart, cover their left eyes, and read the letters to you. Then have them cover their right eyes and read the chart. Which friend could read the most letters?

Was your conclusion correct?

EYE CHART

E
N Z
Y L V
U F V P
N R T S F
O C L G T R
U P N E S R H
T O R E G H B P
F N E G H B S C R
T V H P R U C F N G

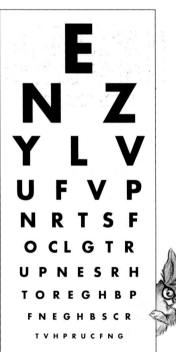